LOOK OUT FOR LITTLE KNIGHT

WRITTEN BY MICHÈLE DUFRESNE · ILLUSTRATED BY MAX STASIUK

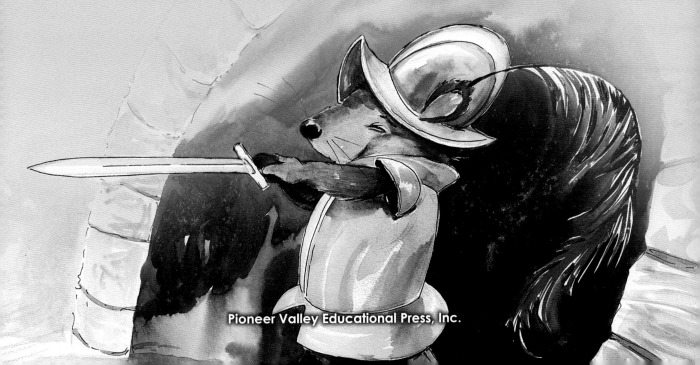

Pioneer Valley Educational Press, Inc.

"Here is my helmet,"
said Little Knight.

2

3

"Here is my armor,"
said Little Knight.

"Look! Here is my sword,"
said Little Knight.

6

"Look at me,"
said Little Knight.
"I am a knight!"

"Look out, cat,"
said Little Knight.

"Look out! Here I come!"